A Note to Parents and Caregivers:

Read-it! Joke Books are for children who are moving ahead on the amazing road to reading. These fun books support the acquisition and extension of reading skills as well as a love of books.

Published by the same company that produces *Read-it!* Readers, these books introduce the question/answer pattern that helps children expand their thinking about language structure and book formats.

When sharing a book with your child, read in short stretches, pausing often to talk about the pictures and the meaning of the book. The question/answer format works well for this purpose and provides an opportunity to talk about the language and meaning of the jokes. Have your child turn the pages and point to the pictures and familiar words. Read the story in a natural voice; have fun creating the voices of characters or emphasizing some important words. And be sure to reread favorite parts.

There is no right or wrong way to share books with children. Find time to read with your child, and pass on the legacy of literacy.

Adria F. Klein, Ph.D.
Professor Emeritus
California State University
San Bernardino, California

Managing Editor: Bob Temple

Creative Director: Terri Foley

Editor: Sara E. Hoffmann

Designer: John Moldstad

Page production: Picture Window Books

The illustrations in this book were prepared digitally.

Picture Window Books

5115 Excelsior Boulevard

Suite 232

Minneapolis, MN 55416

1-877-845-8392

www.picturewindowbooks.com

Printed in the United States of America.

Library of Congress Cataloging-in-Publication Data

Dahl, Michael.

Funny talk : a book of chitchat riddles / written by Michael Dahl ;

illustrated by Ned Shaw.

p. cm. — (Read-it! joke books)

Summary: A collection of riddles about what one object said to another.

ISBN 1-4048-0229-0

1. Riddles, Juvenile. 2. Riddles.

I. Shaw, Ned, ill. II. Title.

PN6371.5 .D344 2004

818'.602—dc21

2003014336

Funny Talk

A Book of Silly Riddles

Michael Dahl • Illustrated by Ned Shaw

Reading Advisers:
Adria F. Klein, Ph.D.
Professor Emeritus, California State University
San Bernardino, California

Susan Kesselring, M.A., Literacy Educator
Rosemount-Apple Valley-Eagan (Minnesota) School District

 Pi

What did the wall say to the other wall?

"Meet me at the corner."

What did the envelope say to the stamp?

6   "Stick with me, and we'll go places."

What did the muffin say to the loaf of bread?

"Must be nice having all that dough." 7

What did the jack say to the car?

"May I give you a lift?"

What did the beaver
say to the tree?

"It's been nice gnawing you."

What did the rug
say to the floor?

10

"Don't move! I've got you covered!"   11

What did the honey bee say to the rose?

"Hi there, bud!"

What did one strawberry say to the other strawberry?

"We're in a jam."

What did the necktie say to the hat?

"You go on a head,
I'll hang around for a while."

What did the firecracker say to the other firecracker?

"My pop is bigger than your pop!"   15

What did one pig
say to another pig?

"Let's be pen pals."

What did the dirt
say to the rain?

"If this keeps up,
my name will be mud."

What did the picture say to the wall?

"I've been framed!"

What did the soccer ball say to the soccer player?

"I get a kick out of you!"

What did the baby porcupine say to the cactus?

"Mommy?"

What did the mother broom say to the baby broom?

"Go to sweep, baby."